MIK'S
MAMMOTH

ROY GERRARD

FARRAR, STRAUS & GIROUX
NEW YORK

Mik the caveman, small and thin,
Had long blond hair and beardless chin.
When danger loomed he saved his skin
By hiding in the cave.
The thought of fighting made him droop,
So other members of the group
Considered him a nincompoop,
For they were fierce and brave.

But food was scarce, and one bleak day
The tribe packed up and went away
To hunt elsewhere, not knowing they
Were leaving Mik behind.
He'd gone exploring far below,
Down where the silver birch trees grow,
And there, among the deep soft snow,
He made the strangest find.

The baby beast was in a mess
And looked at him in deep distress.
Despite his fear, Mik nonetheless
Set to, and dug it out.
When finally the beast was free,
It grew as frisky as could be,
Galumphed around, and squealed with glee
And followed Mik about.

They traveled homeward side by side
To find the cave unoccupied.
Poor Mik sat in the snow and cried,
Beside himself with fear.
But when the snow began to fall,
He dried his tears and built a wall
Around the cave, which, all in all,
Seemed quite a good idea.

Then, safe within their barricade,
They felt completely unafraid.
Mik struck some sparks: a fire was made,
Which cheered them up no end.
The branches blazed so warm and bright
It helped them to forget their plight,
And there Mik spent a cozy night
With Rumm, his newfound friend.

Next day they foraged in the wood,
Found berries there which tasted good,
And roots which made (when cleaned of mud)
A culinary treat.
The tribe would have been most surprised
To see that Mik, whom they despised,
Had used his wits and recognized
That plants were good to eat.

So winter passed and spring came round.
Then, near the cave one day, Mik found
Some seeds he'd scattered on the ground
        Had taken root and grown.
Perfecting first of all the spade,
He went to work, and with Rumm's aid
He dug and delved, and soon he'd made
        A garden of his own.

With food in plenty, they survived
Until the fairer days arrived.
Thus man and beast stood firm and thrived
In friendly harmony.
When summer warmed the countryside,
Rumm grew too big to sleep inside.
He sometimes took Mik for a ride,
So broad and strong was he.

One day a fierce unfriendly bear
Attacked the unsuspecting pair.
He thought their cave could be his lair —
He quickly changed his mind.
Rumm roared and stamped his massive feet,
At which the bear beat swift retreat,
Deciding he'd no wish to meet
A creature of this kind.

Mik found a lake and took a swim.
Then, acting on a sudden whim,
He caught some fish, which seemed to him
    An appetizing meal.
When offered fish, Rumm shook his head
But ate some lily pads instead —
And soon they felt quite overfed
    (They'd gobbled a good deal).

Beside the lake they found some clay
Of reddish-brown and bluey-gray,
Which Mik took home without delay
To try a bright idea.
His clever trick was first of all
To roll the clay into a ball.
With this he drew things on the wall,
Like bison, bears, and deer.

He crushed some berries to produce
Some red and blue and purple juice,
And then he put them all to use
By painting his design.
His little nimble fingers flew,
And though it took him weeks to do,
Eventually, when he was through,
The cave looked really fine.

And then one day, to Mik's delight,
His former friends came into sight
And ran in panic-stricken flight
Toward his cozy den.
He wondered why they made such haste,
Then saw that they were being chased
Across the wild and rocky waste
By hordes of hairy men.

The sight filled Mik with great alarm,
But, keen to save his friends from harm,
He kept his cool, remaining calm,
And leapt on Rumm's broad back.
Toward the savage tribe they sped,
But, happily, no blood was shed —
The hairy horde just turned and fled
When faced by this attack.

The tribe poured praise on Mik and Rumm,
Their hero and his hairy chum,
And all agreed Mik should become
Their leader from that day.
And this is where the story ends:
Mik reunited with his friends,
Who found a way to make amends
For losing him that way.

The moral is that little chaps
May overcome life's handicaps,
And, with some effort, they perhaps
Can triumph in the end.
For Mik won through on brains and wit,
Though fortunate, I must admit,
To have one priceless benefit —
A mammoth for a friend.

First published in Great Britain
by Victor Gollancz Ltd, 1990
Library of Congress catalog card number: 90-55189
Printed in Hong Kong for Imago Publishing Ltd
First American edition, 1990